THE EYES IN THE DARK 2

M. OMAR QURESHI

Made with ♥ on the Notion Press Platform
www.notionpress.com

Contents

I

Recap

In the enthralling saga of the first volume of "*THE EYES IN THE DARK*," a gripping narrative unfolds, weaving together the tales of four intrepid young adventurers thrust into a harrowing quest against the backdrop of the dense Maine jungle in 1978. Led by the indomitable spirit of 14-year-old Emma, whose boundless thirst for adventure fuels their expedition, the quartet is comprised of Eli, a towering and curious soul drawn inexorably to the enigmas of crime and investigation at the age of 14; Amelia, possessed of a keen eye for capturing the world's essence through her photography lens at the age of 13; and Josh, whose unwavering confidence and courage serve as the group's guiding light through the darkest of trials, aged 15.

Their tranquil hometown of Crestwood is plunged into turmoil by the arrival of the malevolent nightstalkers, nocturnal entities shrouded in darkness, who emerge to wreak havoc under the cover of night, assuming the forms of cherished loved ones to lure unsuspecting victims into their grasp. Armed with determination and a relic of ancient power—the fabled Shadow Idol, rumored to be the only weapon capable of quelling the nightstalkers‘ rampage—the quartet embarks on a perilous journey into the heart of the jungle.

Along their path, they encounter a motley array of characters, some claiming friendship but harboring sinister intentions, seeking to manipulate the quartet for their own nefarious ends. Unbeknownst to our heroes, their adversaries seek not to vanquish the nightstalkers, but to harness their dark power, envisioning a future where they reign supreme.

As betrayals unfold and alliances crumble amidst the treacherous foliage, the quartet faces their greatest trial yet, confronting the ultimate test of loyalty and resolve. In a climactic showdown, where the forces of light and shadow clash in a fierce battle for supremacy, the trio of traitors meets their well-deserved fate, while the valiant quartet emerges victorious, hailed as heroes by a grateful world.

Yet, victory comes at a heavy cost, as Eli, stalwart companion and beacon of intellect, succumbs to mortal wounds sustained in the heat of battle, leaving a void in the hearts of his comrades as they return home, forever altered by their epic odyssey into the unknown.

In the wake of their youthful triumph over the nightstalkers in 1978, the passage of time has seen our heroes mature into young adults, their lives shaped by the echoes of their past adventures. As 1982 dawns, a shadow looms once more over the world, as whispers of a resurgence in nightstalker activity ripple through the collective consciousness.

Emma, now 18, a seasoned explorer and leader in her own right, stands at the forefront of the renewed battle against the encroaching darkness. Determined to honor the memory of her fallen comrade Eli and safeguard the world from the nightstalkers' malevolence, she rallies her companions once more.

Eli's absence is keenly felt, his intellect and insight sorely missed in the face of this new threat. Yet, his legacy lives on in the resolve of his friends, who carry his memory in their hearts as they confront the ever-growing darkness.

Amelia's artistic eye now serves not only as a tool for capturing the beauty of the world but also as a means of unmasking the hidden truths that lie beneath the surface. Her photographs become a beacon of hope in the fight against the nightstalkers, revealing their presence where others see only shadows, being now 17 years old.

Josh, now 19 emboldened by past victories and tempered by loss, steps into his role as protector with newfound determination. His courage serves as a pillar of strength for the group, inspiring them to stand firm in the face of adversity.

As the nightstalkers' power grows, threatening to engulf the world in eternal darkness, our heroes must once again venture into the unknown, confronting their fears and forging new alliances in the battle for humanity's survival.

II

Shadows Reawakened

A lazy snowy morning enveloped Crestwood, casting a tranquil blanket over the quaint town. Emma lounged comfortably at home, the weight of impending decisions about her future education weighing on her mind as she sifted through college leaflets with casual deliberation.

Her father, drawn by the allure of the television's glow, entered the room and switched on the news, instantly capturing the attention of everyone in the household. The room fell silent as the reporter's voice echoed through the living room, delivering chilling tidings from Washington DC.

"News coming from Washington DC this morning," the reporter's voice quavered with gravity, "as the capital was violently attacked by humanoid creatures last night, leading to bloodshed." Emma's heart quickened with alarm, her gaze fixed on the screen as the unfolding events seized her attention.

"As the police investigates this further," the reporter continued, "President Ronald Reagan has been successfully and safely evacuated to the west coast." A collective gasp escaped the lips of Emma and her family, the implications of the attack sending shivers down their spines.

"To people living in the states of Maine, Vermont, New Hampshire, Massachusetts, New York, Rhode Island, Connecticut, New Jersey... all the way to Florida and surrounding places," the reporter's words resonated with urgency, "have been ordered to stay home between 6 PM to 10 AM."

Emma's voice trembled with shock as she processed the chilling news. "Wha- What do they mean by humanoid figures?!" Her mind raced, grasping for understanding, until a chilling realization struck her with a force akin to lightning.

Four years ago, they had faced a similar terror. The memory surged forth, unbidden yet vivid, as Emma whispered in a hushed tone, barely audible beneath her breath. "The- The nightstalkers..."

The mere mention of their name sent a shiver down her spine, resurrecting memories of their previous encounter and the harrowing battles they had fought to survive. The sinister creatures, lurking in the shadows, had haunted their every step, their malevolent presence casting a pall over their once-peaceful town.

As the gravity of the situation sank in, Emma's resolve hardened, her fear transforming into steely determination. She knew that they could not afford to underestimate the threat posed by the nightstalkers, nor could they afford to wait for someone else to come to their aid.

With a sense of urgency fueling her actions, Emma rose from her seat, her gaze steely and unwavering. "We can't just sit here and do nothing," she declared, her voice tinged with conviction. "We need to do something. Now."

As Emma rushed to dial Josh and Amelia, her heart pounded with urgency, the distance that time had carved between them melting away in the face of the looming threat. Each ring of the telephone felt like an eternity as she prayed for her friends to answer, her mind racing with plans and possibilities.

Meanwhile, her father, attuned to the severity of the situation, switched channels once more, seeking further insight into the unfolding crisis. The screen flickered to life with the image of a French reporter, their words echoing through the room in a foreign tongue.

"Attaque de créatures impitoyables ? Quels sont-ils?" The words hung in the air, a stark reminder that the horrors unfolding in Washington DC were not isolated to one corner of the globe. Emma's breath caught in her throat as she listened, the gravity of the situation sinking in with each passing moment.

The realization struck her like a bolt of lightning—this time, the threat was not confined to their small town or even their country. It was a global phenomenon, an existential threat that knew no borders.

"खतरनाक जीवों ने कयिा भारत पे हम्ला. क्या चीज़े हैं ये?" The urgent tones of the Hindi reporter added another layer of dread to the unfolding crisis, as Emma struggled to comprehend the full scope of the attacks.

"Атака теней: это американская хитрость?" The Soviet reporter's words only served to deepen the sense of foreboding, as the gravity of the situation became increasingly apparent.

With each new piece of information, Emma felt a knot tightening in her chest, the weight of the world's fear pressing down upon her shoulders. Yet, amidst the chaos and uncertainty, she knew that she could not afford to succumb to despair.

Drawing upon the strength of her resolve, Emma steeled herself for the challenges that lay ahead. The world may be reeling from the onslaught of the nightstalkers, but she refused to be paralyzed by fear. Together with her friends and allies, she would stand as a beacon of hope in the face of darkness, determined to confront the shadows and restore peace to a world gripped by chaos.

Calling up others, she scheduled an emergency meeting at her house. Soon, Josh and Amelia arrived, with Amelia having the book about these creatures. *

* = see THE EYES IN THE DARK volume 1

III

End of the World?

As they gathered in Emma's room, the weight of the world's turmoil heavy upon their shoulders, a sudden voice from the radio pierced the air, drawing their attention with its urgent tone.

"Scientists of the world have been intrigued by an unexplainable amount of energy being released from an area deep within the jungles of Maine," the reporter's voice crackled through the static, sending a chill down their spines. "An expedition and a helicopter search over the area found a destroyed structure of what seemed to be a temple with ancient carvings."

Emma and her companions exchanged incredulous glances as the reporter's words sank in. The discovery of the ancient temple in their very own backyard sent shockwaves through their group, each one grappling with the implications of such a profound revelation.

"Legend says that a sacred idol is the safekeeper of the temple, which if exits the premises caused the temple to collapse," the reporter continued, his words sending a shiver down their spines.

"The shadow idol has been stolen!" Amelia's voice rang out, her eyes wide with alarm. The realization hit them like a thunderbolt, the gravity of the situation becoming all too clear.

"Do you think we should go back to the temple?" she asked, her voice trembling with uncertainty.

Emma shook her head, her expression resolute. "No chance," she replied firmly. "It is safely guarded by the military as the scientists explore it. Besides that, we don't know where the idol could be or who took it."

The room fell silent as they absorbed Emma's words, the enormity of their predicament weighing heavily upon them. But even in the face of uncertainty, they knew that they could not afford to lose hope. With their resolve strengthened by adversity, they vowed to stand united against the darkness, ready to confront whatever challenges lay ahead in their quest to reclaim the shadow idol and restore balance to their world.

Opening the book, the weathered pages revealed a cryptic warning:

"If one makes peace with the nightstalkers by offering them the sacred idol, they shall ascend as the leader, wielding unimaginable power to shape the fate of civilizations. However, this path leads only to ruin. The sole means to avert catastrophe is to safely return the idol to its rightful place within the temple."

Reading further, an eerie poem made them uneasy

"In the crimson dusk, shadows dance, As nightstalkers rise in their malevolent trance. The sky aglow with a blood-red hue, An omen of terror, a harbinger true.

Beneath the veil of night's dark shroud, Their whispers echo, chilling and loud. A fury unleashed, a symphony of screams, As nightmares awaken from fitful dreams.

With each crimson hue, their power grows, A legion of darkness, no mercy bestows. Through the veil of twilight, they emerge, To sow chaos and death, their unholy surge.

Beware the sky, stained with blood-red stain, For the nightstalkers' wrath shall leave no domain. In shadows they dwell, in darkness they thrive, A chilling reminder of the price to survive."

IV
Pattern

Josh's encounter with the newspaper vendor sparks a brilliant idea, and as he returns to Emma's house with a stack of newspapers, he wastes no time in sharing his revelation with Amelia.

Amelia, intrigued by Josh's urgency, listens intently as he lays out the newspapers on the table before them. With each headline detailing a different attack by the nightstalkers, Amelia begins to see the threads connecting them all.

"There must be a pattern in where in the world these attacks happened," Josh asserts, his eyes alight with determination.

Amelia nods in agreement, her mind already racing ahead. Without hesitation, she retrieves a world map and a handful of thumbtacks, spreading them out before Josh.

"Here, mark the locations of the attacks as mentioned in the newspapers," she instructs, her voice steady and focused.

As Josh meticulously marks each city on the map, the pattern becomes increasingly clear. With each thumbtack, the trail of destruction left by the nightstalkers is laid bare before them.

"The first attack happened in Vladivostok, Soviet Union," Josh explains, his voice tinged with urgency as he places the first thumbtack on the map.

Amelia nods in agreement, her eyes scanning the map as Josh continues to add more thumbtacks, tracing the path of the attacks across continents and time zones.

"Next, here is Pyongyang, Seoul, Beijing, Shanghai," he continues, his fingers moving with purpose as he adds each new city to the map.

"There's Kathmandu, Bombay, Delhi, and Calcutta," Emma chimes in, her voice steady as she joins Josh in marking the map with thumbtacks.

"Dubai, Damascus, Ankara, Istanbul, Paris, and Washington DC," Josh concludes, his gaze lingering on the map before them. "Those are all the cities attacked till now."

As they stand before the map, the gravity of their discovery weighs heavily upon them. Each thumbtack represents a city besieged by the nightstalkers, a testament to the scale of the threat they face.

As they scrutinize the map, Amelia prompts the group with a question, "Did anyone else notice something about the pattern?"

Josh, always quick to contribute, asserts, "The cities seem to align in a straight line, don't they?"

Amelia, in a teasing tone, remarks, "Even I caught onto that, you dummy"

Meanwhile, Emma interjects with a sudden insight, "Hold on, let's think about this. The Earth rotates counterclockwise, right? So, if you look at the cities from Vladivostok to Washington DC, they form a straight line. That implies the attacks moved westward, trailing the night."

Josh, feeling misunderstood, clarifies, "Hey, that's what I was trying to say!"

Amelia, determined to maintain focus, intervenes firmly, pressing her hand against Josh's mouth to silence him and refocusing the group's attention on the task at hand.

With tensions momentarily diffused, they continue to dissect the pattern of attacks, each member contributing their insights and observations. In the midst of their discussion, a sense of urgency builds—a realization dawns that they may be closer to uncovering the truth behind the nightstalkers' nefarious agenda than they ever imagined.

In a sudden burst of realization, Josh pushes Amelia's hand away, determined to share his insight. "Wait, if the previous attack was at DC and the attacks move west, then the next attack is going to be at..." His words are cut short as the night sky abruptly turns a menacing shade of red, drowned out by the cacophony of terrifying screeches filling the air.

"Run," Emma's urgent command pierces through the chaos as she peers out the window, witnessing the nightstalkers descending from the crimson sky, unleashing chaos upon the unsuspecting populace below.

"Turn on all the lights!" Amelia's voice rises above the turmoil, her command echoing through Emma's house as others scramble to follow suit, desperately seeking refuge in the piercing glow of artificial illumination.

V

Attack of the Nightstalkers

As the ground trembled and the lights flickered ominously, the house was abruptly engulfed in darkness as the lamps extinguished. The power grid had been decimated. "Now I understand why they are such big cheeses," Josh murmured aloud as they took refuge in the basement with Emma's parents, the only place in the house with an auxiliary power supply.

"Ow!!" Josh yelped as Emma kicked his leg, annoyed by his poorly timed remark.

They huddled together, anxiety hanging heavily in the air. The nightstalkers—towering seven to eight-foot-tall shadowy humanoid figures with glinting eyes, bloodthirsty minds, and elongated teeth, aptly named the Eyes in the Dark—rampaged through their house, scouring for any survivors.

The basement door quaked under the nightstalkers' relentless assault. Eerie, bloodcurdling screeches reverberated through the basement as the nightstalkers sniffed out their quarry, pounding furiously on the door in their attempt to breach it. The group held their breath, praying the reinforced door would withstand the relentless onslaught of the monstrous beings outside.

Eventually, the door gave way, crashing down and nearly striking Emma's mom. Emma's dad sprang to his feet, determined to protect his family. Armed with an automatic rifle, he fired a barrage of bullets at the nightstalkers at the door, but his efforts were futile. The adult nightstalkers, with their uncanny ability to evade gunfire and other attacks, advanced unharmed.

As the creatures closed in, poised to pounce, their only source of light flickered ominously. In a desperate move, Amelia jumped forward and shone a flashlight directly into the nightstalkers' faces. The sudden burst of light startled the creatures, driving them back and providing a crucial moment of reprieve for the beleaguered family.

As the attacks subsided and the creatures moved west away from the rising sun, the family cautiously emerged from the basement. The once quiet town of Crestwood lay in ruins. Though the infrastructure remained intact, the streets were filled with the cries of the wounded and the grieving, blood mingling with the snow, transforming the serene landscape into a scene of horror.

Amelia and Josh quickly called their homes, relieved to find that the telephone lines were still operational and their parents were unharmed. The relief was palpable, but the devastation around them was undeniable.

Soon, the distinctive "thwomp thwomp" of helicopter rotors echoed in the distance. A convoy of military and press helicopters descended upon the town, landing on the streets and hovering above the blood-stained snow. Soldiers and reporters disembarked, surveying the aftermath of the nightstalkers' rampage, ready to offer aid and document the tragedy that had befallen Crestwood.

VI

Off on adventure

As they continued to analyze the patterns of the attacks, Josh spoke up with a sudden realization. "The attacks began at Vladivostok... I think the idol is there!"

Amelia, skeptical, replied, "How are you so sure?"

Josh explained, "Well, think from the leader's perspective. If you were the leader of the nightstalkers, where would you attack first?"

Amelia fell silent, contemplating Josh's reasoning.

Emma, deep in thought, said, "Hmm, let's say I was in Madrid. I'd probably start the attack there itself because I wouldn't have to calculate what time it is in other cities around the world." She paused, the significance of her own words dawning on her. "JOSH, YOU'RE A GENIUS!"

"Oh yeah, that I am," Josh replied confidently, smiling broadly.

Emma, however, couldn't resist teasing him. "Calm down, Smartypants. This is the only time you've been useful," she sneered, causing Josh's smile to fade into a look of disappointment.

"Awwh," he said, his enthusiasm dampened.

"Okay, Albert Einstein, let's suppose the idol is at Vladivostok. How are we supposed to get there?" asked Amelia.

"We fly the—" Josh began, only to be abruptly interrupted by Amelia slapping a sheet of newspaper against his face.

"What the hell, Ami?" Josh exclaimed, demanding an explanation.

With a swift kick to his knee, Amelia replied, "How many times have I told you not to call me that?" Josh fell to the ground, clutching his knee.

Standing over him, Amelia handed him the newspaper. "Read it!"

Josh, still smarting from the kick, took the newspaper and read aloud, "Brezhnev orders complete closure of border. All aircraft to and from the Soviet Union to pause operations due to ongoing crisis, as Moscow stated."

The others listened intently, absorbing the grim news. Emma, deep in thought, began considering alternative ways to reach Vladivostok despite the daunting obstacles ahead. They needed a new plan.

"Well, we can go to North Korea and then cross the border into Russia!" Josh suggested, positive that the plan would work.

"Really?" Emma responded, giving him a skeptical glance. "North Korea?"

Josh's confidence wavered under Emma's scrutiny. "Yeah, you know what, scratch that," he replied, feeling a bit embarrassed by his suggestion.

The group fell silent, pondering their next move. The path to Vladivostok seemed increasingly complicated, and they needed a more viable solution to reach their destination.

"I know!" Emma broke the silence. "We sneak onto a humanitarian aid plane going to the Soviet Union!"

Josh raised an eyebrow and replied, "And I believe the -94 Fahrenheit temperatures at 40,000 feet and lack of oxygen would take care of itself?"

Emma sighed, realizing the impracticality of her suggestion. "Okay, maybe sneaking onto a plane isn't the best idea. But what if we contact a humanitarian organization directly? They might need volunteers, and we could join one of their convoys legally."

Amelia nodded, considering the idea. "That could work. We just need to find a way to convince them that we're essential for their mission."

Emma's dad interjected, "I might have a contact who can help. An old friend in the military is involved in coordinating relief efforts. If I explain our situation, he might be able to get us on one of those planes as official volunteers."

The group exchanged hopeful glances as Emma's dad picked up the phone and dialed his friend. After a tense conversation, he hung up and turned to them with a determined look.

"He can get us on a humanitarian aid flight heading to Vladivostok. We need to move quickly and be ready to leave at a moment's notice."

Josh grinned. "Looks like we have a plan. Let's pack up and get ready. We're going to Vladivostok."

The group quickly gathered their belongings, mentally preparing for the next leg of their perilous journey, hoping this plan would bring them one step closer to Vladivostok and the shadow idol.

As the day dawned, casting a pale light over the airfield in Washington, the group made their way across the tarmac, their breath condensing in the frigid air, a visible reminder of the biting cold. Arriving at the waiting C-130J Super Hercules, they could feel the rumble of the engines beneath their feet as they climbed aboard.

Taking their seats along the wall-mounted benches, they glanced around at the interior of the aircraft, the UN cargo stacked neatly in front of them. The air inside was chilly, but they knew it would be nothing compared to the freezing temperatures awaiting them at 40,000 feet.

As the engines roared to life and the plane taxied down the runway, they braced themselves for the journey ahead, their hearts filled with a mixture of trepidation and determination. They were bound for Vladivostok, ready to confront whatever challenges lay in their path in their quest to retrieve the shadow idol and put an end to the nightstalkers' reign of terror.

"Ugh, how long is this gonna take!?" complained Amelia, her frustration evident as she shifted uncomfortably in her seat.

"Ami..." Emma began tentatively, but she was silenced by the intense glare from Amelia. Clearing her throat, Emma corrected herself, "I mean, Amelia, we just took off and we have... uh, 15 more hours to go."

"Ahhh, gosh darn it!" Amelia screamed in exasperation, her outburst drawing uneasy glances from the other passengers. She was quickly shushed by the group, reminded of the need to maintain a low profile during their covert journey.

As the hours stretched ahead of them, the group settled in for the long flight, their anticipation mounting with each passing minute. They knew that every second brought them closer to their destination and the daunting challenges awaiting them in Vladivostok.

After 15 grueling hours, the distant outline of land finally came into view as the plane descended into Vladivostok. Exhausted from the long journey, Josh had drifted off to sleep, only to wake up with both Emma and Amelia snoozing on his shoulder.

Annoyed by their weight, Josh shrugged them off, causing Emma to startle awake and accidentally deliver a tight slap to his cheek in her disoriented state.

"Shoot! Sorry!" Emma exclaimed, her eyes wide with alarm as she realized what she had done.

"Don't mention it," Josh replied skeptically, rubbing his reddened cheek where Emma's slap had landed. Despite his attempt to brush it off, the sting of the slap lingered, adding to the discomfort of their already tumultuous journey.

Eventually, the plane touched down at Vladivostok International Airport, bringing an end to its long and tumultuous journey. As the cabin doors opened, a blast of frigid, frozen air swept through the aircraft, causing the group to shiver involuntarily as they disembarked onto the icy tarmac.

Stepping onto Russian soil, they were greeted by the sight of snow-covered landscapes stretching as far as the eye could see. Despite the biting cold, there was a sense of relief and anticipation among the group as they prepared to embark on the next phase of their mission.

The airport staff, bundled up in heavy coats and hats, hurriedly assisted the team in deplaning the cargo, eager to unload the humanitarian aid supplies and get the aircraft ready for its next flight. Amidst the flurry of activity, the group exchanged determined looks, ready to face whatever challenges lay ahead in their quest to locate the shadow idol and put an end to the nightstalkers' reign of terror.

"Oi!" The trio heard someone calling out. "OI!" the voice shouted louder, catching their attention. "Whoever he's calling is in trouble," remarked Amelia, her eyes scanning the bustling airport terminal.

The source of the voice, a burly man with a thick Russian accent, approached them with purpose. With a light tap on the head of each of them, he gruffly spoke, "Oi, you Americans, deaf? Khave you done za immigration? Go zere!" He pointed towards the immigration counters, his tone leaving no room for argument.

Feeling a mixture of irritation and amusement at the man's brusque demeanor, the trio nodded in acknowledgment and made their way towards the designated area. It was clear that navigating their way through the bureaucratic hurdles of immigration would be just the first of many challenges they would face in Vladivostok.

VII

Vladivostok

As Josh stepped up to the officer, the man inquired gruffly, "Name, date of za birth, broffession, burboze ov visit?"

An awkward moment ensued as Josh replied nervously, "Josh, 12/3/1963, uh, jobless, trying to get the shadow ido- I mean to deliver humanitarian aid," he trailed off, a nervous smile forming on his lips as sweat beaded on his forehead.

"My friend, you look like you see ghost! Sit down. Want vodka?" the officer offered, his tone surprisingly friendly despite his intimidating appearance.

"Yeah, no thanks, I- I don't drink," Josh declined politely, his nerves still on edge.

The smile on the officer's face faltered momentarily. "Oh," he muttered, before abruptly walking away muttering "pridurok," calling him a jerk in Russian.

Josh couldn't help but feel a bit uneasy as he watched the officer depart, uncertain of what awaited them next in this unfamiliar land.

The officer returned, handing Josh a glass bottle filled with a dark, carbonated liquid adorned with Russian writing. "Uh... wha-what's this?" Josh inquired, eyeing the unfamiliar beverage with suspicion.

"Baikal," the guard replied proudly.

"Baikal?" Repeated Josh, puzzled by the name

"Da, Baikal. This Soviet Coca Cola. Better quality, made in Russia!" he added, his chest puffing out with pride at the mention of the locally produced soda.

Josh cautiously took a sip, half-expecting the drink to be poisoned. "Come on, my friend! Drink freely. I haven't poisoned it!" the guard chuckled, his laughter echoing through the terminal.

As Josh hesitated, the guard leaned in closer, his voice dropping to a whisper. "Well, I would've if you didn't come with da aid," he admitted with a sly grin.

"What was that?" Josh asked, his concern mounting at the guard's cryptic remark.

"Uhh... nothing!" the guard quickly backtracked, his expression shifting to one of innocence as he briskly walked away, leaving Josh to ponder the unsettling encounter.

Josh emerged from the terminal, a crate of Baikals in hand, and distributed the bottles to his team and the weary travelers as they boarded the waiting bus, heading downtown.

As they drove through the city streets, the devastation wrought by the nightstalkers' attacks was painfully evident. Blood-stained ruins stood as grim reminders of the horrors that had unfolded here. Yet, amidst the destruction, there was a sense of hope and resilience in the air.

People gathered around as the aid trucks and buses arrived, their faces lighting up with relief at the sight of much-needed supplies. Josh and his team wasted no time in unloading the crates of Baikal and other essentials, eager to provide assistance to those in need.

As they walked the streets, Amelia's sharp eyes caught sight of a group of Soviet soldiers huddled in a corner. Clad in black ushankas adorned with a proud red star and armed with assault rifles, they bore the marks of battle, their uniforms stained with blood and dirt. Amelia couldn't help but feel a sense of unease as she observed them, wondering what their presence meant for their mission in Vladivostok.

Coming close to Amelia and Emma, Josh inquired, "When do we make a run?"

"Obviously not right now! We're surrounded and can't do anything," Amelia and Emma said in unison, their voices echoing each other's words.

They glanced at each other, sharing a smile before speaking in unison once again. "Hey, we said it together!"

"Ok, jokes aside..." said Josh, prompting Emma to put a finger to his lips and causing him to pause mid-sentence. Puzzled, he opened his mouth to ask what happened, then realization dawned on him, causing Emma to chuckle, her breath condensing in the cold air.

"Ok, now let's get serious. What do we do?" Josh asked, his tone more earnest this time.

"HEY YOU THREE!" shouted someone nearby, interrupting Amelia as she attempted to outline her plan. The man continued, "What are you three doing there, strategizing a game or something? Come help!"

"How did you know?" replied Amelia jokingly, a playful grin on her face, causing the man to roll his eyes before continuing on to carry the crate.

As the group continued their conversation, Amelia retrieved the itinerary provided for their trip. Clearing her throat, she read aloud, "Day 4: Have breakfast and explore the surroundings. The workers are free to walk around and explore the city one day before departure for back home.

They cannot exit the district of Vladivostok nor go near forbidden locations like the border of North Korea."

Josh furrowed his brow in thought. "So, we have a day to explore Vladivostok before we head back home. That should give us some time to gather information and scout out potential leads on the shadow idol."

Amelia nodded in agreement. "Exactly. We'll need to be strategic about where we go and who we talk to. We don't want to draw unnecessary attention to ourselves, especially considering the restrictions outlined in the itinerary."

Emma chimed in, her eyes bright with determination. "Let's make the most of this opportunity. We'll divide and conquer, covering as much ground as possible while staying within the designated boundaries. With any luck, we'll uncover some valuable clues that will lead us closer to finding the shadow idol."

As the days passed, the group dedicated themselves to assisting the people of Vladivostok, providing aid and support to those in need. Their efforts did not go unnoticed, and soon the residents of the city expressed their gratitude for the assistance they had received.

Despite their growing rapport with the locals, the group remained cautious about discussing sensitive matters, especially over the telephone. Emma hesitated to share any updates about their search for the idol with her father back home in the USA. Telephoning from the Soviet Union to the USA during the height of the Cold War posed a significant risk of their communications being intercepted or monitored by authorities.

Aware of the potential consequences of speaking openly about their mission, Emma chose her words carefully, focusing instead on reassurances of their safety and well-being. It was a delicate balancing act, navigating their desire to maintain secrecy while keeping their loved ones informed about their activities abroad.

As they continued their quest for the shadow idol amidst the backdrop of geopolitical tensions, the group remained ever vigilant, mindful of the dangers that lurked in the shadows of Vladivostok.

As the night of day 3 descended upon Vladivostok, the group and their fellow volunteers gathered around a crackling fire, exchanging stories and sharing moments of camaraderie. The flickering flames cast dancing shadows across their faces as they listened intently to each other's tales.

Amidst the laughter and camaraderie, the hushed tones of a radio broadcast caught everyone's attention. The announcer's voice echoed through the night air, delivering somber news of the escalating onslaught of the shadow creatures.

"Now, Radio Seoul is bringing you the news about the increased onslaught of the shadow creatures," the broadcast began, listing off a series of cities that had fallen victim to the nightmarish attacks. Tokyo, Osaka, Jakarta, Singapore, Kuala Lumpur, Madras, Colombo, Riyadh, Alexandria, Tripoli, Algiers, Tunis, Casablanca, Rabat, Northern Mexico, and Southern USA—all had felt the devastating impact of the relentless onslaught.

"Po...poor souls," a voice from the group murmured, the weight of the news hanging heavy in the air. The gravity of the situation was palpable, and for a moment, the group fell silent, each lost in their own thoughts as they contemplated the horrors unfolding beyond the borders of Vladivostok.

VIII

Dominic

As the group tended to the fire, adding fuel to ward off any potential nightstalkers, Emma's voice cut through the crackling flames. "Another pattern has emerged!" she exclaimed, her words carrying a sense of urgency. Memories of their discussions back home flooded her mind as she pieced together the unfolding events. "The attacks were originally in the north, and now they're moving south. Poor things! There won't be a single city left in the world where they wouldn't have rained hell!"

Josh rose to his feet, his expression determined. "We can't sit and crib over it," he declared, his voice firm with resolve. "There's no use dwelling on the devastation. Tomorrow, we'll set out and find the idol once and for all."

As the morning sun cast its warm glow upon Vladivostok, painting the sky in vibrant hues of orange and yellow, the group rose early, their anticipation palpable as they prepared to embark on another day of exploration. Eager to uncover new discoveries, they gathered for breakfast, the aroma of freshly brewed coffee mingling with the scent of morning dew.

Amidst the chatter and laughter of the volunteers, Josh's keen gaze fell upon the same group of soldiers they had encountered before. Unlike the others, these soldiers seemed to fixate their attention on the trio with an intensity that sent a shiver down Josh's spine. "Something fishy is going on," he declared, his voice low and cautious.

Emma, caught off guard by the sudden declaration, furrowed her brow in confusion. "What?" she asked, her tone tinged with curiosity.

Pointing discreetly towards the soldiers, Josh replied, "The soldiers, look!" His gesture drew Emma's attention to the group, and her eyes widened in realization. Sensing that they had been noticed, a sense of unease washed over the trio as they exchanged nervous glances.

"Yeah, I noticed them too," Emma whispered, her voice tinged with apprehension. "They've been acting weird ever since they saw us."

With a sense of foreboding hanging in the air, the group hastily finished their breakfast, their minds racing with questions and concerns about the soldiers' peculiar behavior. Little did they know, their encounter with the soldiers would set off a chain of events that would thrust them deeper into the heart of the mystery surrounding the shadow idol.

As they roamed the streets of Vladivostok, clad in attire meant to signify their neutrality as humanitarian aid workers, the group's search for clues led them deeper into the heart of the city. Despite their best efforts, the streets remained devoid of any promising leads, and frustration began to set in.

"Yep, let's give up," declared Josh, his words heavy with defeat as he voiced the exhaustion and disillusionment gnawing at their resolve.

Emma's reaction was swift and biting, her frustration boiling over as she lashed out at Josh. "Oh, so now you're the one ready to throw in the towel?" she retorted, her voice dripping with sarcasm. "I seem to recall someone preaching about not giving up just yesterday!"

Her taunt struck a nerve, and Josh bristled at her words, his own temper flaring in response. "You think this is a joke?" he snapped, his frustration bubbling to the surface. "We're not getting anywhere with this aimless wandering!"

The tension between them escalated quickly, threatening to erupt into a physical altercation until Amelia stepped in, her voice calm but firm as she intervened to defuse the situation. "Enough," she admonished, her tone brooking no argument. "We're all feeling the pressure, but fighting amongst ourselves won't solve anything. Let's focus on the task at hand and work together to find a solution."

As they ventured deeper into the alleyway, their senses on high alert, Amelia's intuition tingled with the sensation of being watched. Casting a wary glance over her shoulder, she spotted a group of four soldiers lingering in the distance, their gaze fixed upon them as they smoked cigarettes with an air of casual indifference. Despite their nonchalant demeanor, Amelia couldn't shake the feeling of unease that settled in the pit of her stomach.

Moving closer to Josh, who was at the forefront of their group, Amelia attempted to maintain a sense of calm, her eyes darting between the soldiers and her companions. However, her efforts were abruptly interrupted when one of the soldiers stepped forward, blocking their path and demanding to know their identities.

As Amelia waited anxiously for the soldier to release them, a sudden commotion erupted behind her, drawing her attention away from the interrogation. With a sickening thud and a crunch of snow beneath her feet, she turned to find Emma sprawled on the ground, unconscious. Before she could react, a searing pain lanced through her skull, causing her vision to blur and her legs to buckle beneath her.

As the world spun dizzily around her, Amelia heard the soldier's voice pierce through the haze of pain, granting them permission to leave. Confusion and fear clouded Josh's expression as he turned to face his fallen companions, only to be met with a swift and brutal blow to the head that sent him crashing to the ground.

As darkness closed in around them, the soldiers responsible for their incapacitation emerged from the shadows, their mocking laughter echoing through the alleyway as they reveled in their victory.

As Josh's consciousness slowly returned, he found himself lying on the cold, hard ground, his head throbbing with pain. Blinking away the haze of disorientation, he struggled to make sense of his surroundings.

Panic surged through him as he scanned the room, his heart racing with fear and confusion. "Ugh... why am I tied up?!" he exclaimed, his voice laced with urgency as he tried to free himself from his restraints.

To his dismay, Josh soon realized that he was not alone. Nearby, Amelia and Emma stirred from their unconscious state, their groans of discomfort echoing in the dimly lit room. Like him, they were bound and helpless, their predicament mirroring his own.

As the unfamiliar voice pierced the tense silence of the room, Josh's muscles tensed, his heart pounding with apprehension. "Who are you?! Why are we here?!" he demanded, his voice trembling with a mix of fear and defiance as he struggled against his restraints.

The stranger, who introduced himself as Dominic Blaze, regarded them with a cold, calculating gaze, his demeanor betraying no hint of remorse or empathy. "I am Dominic Blaze. Does it sound familliar? I am the son of Tristan Blaze, whom you three murdered!" he hissed, holding the Idol.

"You thief!" Josh spat, his voice dripping with contempt as he strained against his bonds, futilely attempting to reach Dominic.

But their captor showed no mercy, his words dripping with malice as he explained his twisted motives. "My father's death was just the beginning," Dominic sneered, his voice laced with bitterness. "I aim to fulfill his dark desires and exact revenge upon those who wronged him. You three just happened to stumble into my plans."

As Dominic callously dismissed their protests and walked away, leaving them to their fate, Josh's anger boiled over. His desperate attempt to confront their enemy ended in humiliation as he tumbled to the ground, his hopes of escape dwindling with each passing moment. "Well, that didn't go as planned," he muttered, his voice tinged with self-deprecation as he lay there, defeated. He watched helplessly as Dominic walked away, the sound of his laughter echoing in the air.

IX

Escape

As they wrestled against their restraints, the confined space seemed to press in on them, amplifying the urgency of their predicament. Amelia winced, feeling a throbbing ache in her head from the impact of their capture. The discomfort served as a constant reminder of the peril they faced.

In the midst of their struggles, Josh's sudden outcry startled them all. "What's the matter?" Amelia asked, her concern evident as she turned towards him. "MICE!" he exclaimed, a mix of surprise and revulsion coloring his tone. Emma rolled her eyes at his outburst, dismissing it even as a sense of unease lingered in the air.

Amelia felt a subtle movement against her hand, her heart skipping a beat as she realized they were not alone in the room. With a swift motion, she freed her hands from the restraints, the sensation of nibbling ceasing as she did so. Quickly regaining her composure, she moved to untie her legs, her focus sharpened by the imminent threat.

As they prepared for the impending confrontation, the door swung open, revealing the imposing figure of an armed soldier. His chilling words hung in the air, a grim reminder of the danger they faced. "Less suffering for you all," he intoned, his voice cold and devoid of mercy. "You will be devoured by a black bear in this room soon."

Amelia exchanged a knowing glance with Emma, silently acknowledging the sinister intent behind the soldier's words. With a sense of urgency, they worked together to free themselves from their restraints, their movements swift and coordinated.

But as they attempted to escape, they were met with another obstacle—the locked door barring their way to freedom. Josh's eyes darted around the room, searching for a solution, and his gaze fell upon a sturdy tree branch lying nearby. Seizing it with determination, he prepared to confront their would-be captors.

As the soldiers entered the room, their expressions hardened with intent, only to find their quarry gone. In a swift and calculated move, Josh incapacitated all four soldiers one by one. He called out "One, two, three, and four!"

Amelia couldn't help but smile as she watched Josh's triumphant display, his resourcefulness proving to be their saving grace.

As the group spotted the exit, they sprinted towards it, only to be abruptly halted by two swift smacks on the head from Emma. "Don't you remember what we were searching for? We need to find the idol first!" she said, her voice firm, stopping Josh and Amelia in their tracks.

Turning around, the trio cautiously navigated the stronghold, their senses heightened as they tried to locate Dominic. They moved silently through dimly lit corridors, the weight of their mission pressing on them.

Suddenly, they heard Dominic's voice echoing through the halls, calling out in frustration. "Dimitri!" he shouted, unaware that his partners were out cold and locked in a room. "Dimitri, answer me for God's sake!" Dominic's voice grew increasingly irritated.

Stealthily, the trio followed the sound of his voice, inching closer to their goal.

There he sat, behind a glass wall, elegantly waiting for his soldiers to return with the teens to unleash the bear that was now growling in its cage. Dominic's fingers tapped rhythmically on the desk, his expression a mixture of boredom and anticipation.

Josh, Amelia, and Emma carefully approached the glass wall, peeking through a crack in the door. They saw the idol sitting on Dominic's desk, glinting under the dim light. The bear's growls grew louder, making the air thick with tension.

"We need to distract him and grab the idol," Emma whispered, her eyes fixed on the artifact. "I'll create a diversion," Josh volunteered. "You two get ready to grab it."

As Josh prepared to act, Amelia noticed a small control panel on the wall next to the glass. "That must control the bear's cage," she whispered back. "We can use it to our advantage."

Josh nodded, taking a deep breath before stepping into view. "Hey, Dominic!" he shouted, drawing the man's attention. Dominic's head snapped up, eyes narrowing as he spotted Josh.

Before Dominic could react, Emma and Amelia slipped into the room. Amelia rushed to the control panel, while Emma grabbed the idol from the desk.

Dominic's eyes widened in realization. "You little brats!" he bellowed, reaching for his gun.

But before he could draw, Amelia hit the button on the control panel. The bear's cage door flew open, and the beast roared, charging at Dominic.

With the bear as their unintentional ally, the trio dashed out of the room, idol in hand, the sounds of chaos echoing behind them.

Suddenly, as the chaos quieted down, Josh peeked back into the room. His eyes widened in horror at the sight of the bear lying dead on the ground, nightstalkers surrounding its lifeless body, snarling and growling. Dominic, spotting Josh through the crack in the door, immediately commanded the nightstalkers, "GET THEM AND DON'T LET THEM ESCAPE!"

Josh quickly ducked back, his heart pounding. "We've got company," he whispered urgently to Amelia and Emma.

"We need to get out of here now," Amelia said, clutching the idol tightly.

The trio sprinted down the corridor, the sounds of the nightstalkers' growls and Dominic's shouts echoing behind them. They turned corners frantically, searching for a way out of the stronghold.

Emma glanced back, seeing the shadowy figures gaining on them. "They're getting closer!"

Josh spotted a narrow passageway leading to a staircase. "This way!" he shouted, leading them down the stairs. They stumbled through the dark, the nightstalkers hot on their heels.

As they reached the bottom, they found themselves in a dimly lit basement with multiple exits. "We need to split up and confuse them," Amelia suggested, panting heavily. "We'll meet back at the main entrance."

Without wasting another moment, they each took a different exit, hoping to throw off their pursuers. The nightstalkers hesitated briefly, confused by the sudden dispersion, before splitting up to follow each path.

Josh ran through the maze-like corridors, his mind racing. He could hear the nightstalkers behind him, their growls growing louder. Just as he felt their presence closing in, he spotted a door ahead, slightly ajar. He slipped inside and held his breath, listening as the footsteps passed by.

Meanwhile, Amelia and Emma navigated their own paths, using every bit of their agility and wits to avoid capture. Amelia found herself in a storage room, quickly hiding behind crates. Emma, on the other hand, ended up in a maintenance tunnel, crawling through to stay out of sight.

Eventually, the trio managed to shake off their pursuers and reconvened at the main entrance. "Did you guys lose them?" Josh asked, breathless.

"For now," Amelia replied, still clutching the idol. "But we need to get out of here before they regroup."

X

Journey back home

As the group arrived back at the airport, breathless and hiding the idol, the instructor of the plane called them up. "About time! Where were ya'll for so long? Grabbing an idol from some evil guy?!" he shouted, his voice tinged with anger and sarcasm.

"Uhhh, how does he know about it?" Amelia whispered to the group, her eyes wide with confusion.

"Shut up, he's being sarcastic!" Josh replied, trying to keep his voice down.

The trio, still on edge, hurried to board the aircraft. They found their seats and settled in, the adrenaline from their escape still coursing through their veins. As the plane's engines roared to life, they felt a mix of relief and anxiety. The idol was now safely in their possession, but the events in Vladivostok had shaken them deeply.

As they buckled up and prepared for takeoff, Amelia glanced at the idol, its mysterious aura almost palpable. "Do you think we're really safe now?" she asked, her voice barely above a whisper.

Emma sighed, "For now, yes. But we can't let our guard down. Dominic and his nightstalkers won't give up that easily."

Josh nodded in agreement, "We'll need to figure out our next steps once we're back home. For now, let's just focus on getting there."

The plane ascended into the sky, leaving the chaos of Vladivostok behind. As they flew towards home, the trio couldn't help but reflect on their journey, the challenges they had faced, and the dangers that still lay ahead. They knew that their mission was far from over, but they were more determined than ever to see it through to the end.

In the quiet of the plane's cabin, with the hum of the engines lulling them into a semblance of calm, they finally allowed themselves a moment of rest.

As the plane cruised high above the Sea of Okhotsk, the sun set, shrouding the landscape in darkness. "Wait..." said Josh, a dawning realization making his eyes widen in shock. "If it's sundown and now it's dark, does that mean..."

Emma and Amelia exchanged alarmed glances. "B-but they can't fly, right?" Amelia questioned nervously.

Suddenly, loud shrieks echoed outside the plane. Passengers peered out the windows, panic spreading as they caught glimpses of the nightstalkers swarming towards the aircraft.

The nightstalkers began their relentless assault, their clawed limbs tearing at the fuselage. Ordered by Dominic, who knew the trio was onboard, they were determined to bring down the plane. The aircraft shook violently under the onslaught, sending passengers and crew flying. Screams filled the cabin as chaos erupted.

Emma was thrown across the aisle, slamming hard into the opposite side. "OWHH! My back!" she cried out, struggling to rise amid the turmoil.

Josh and Amelia grabbed onto their seats, trying to steady themselves. "We have to do something!" Josh shouted over the deafening noise.

The nightstalkers, now overpowering the aircraft, forced it into a steep descent. The plane hurtled downward, losing altitude at a terrifying rate. The ground below loomed closer, a few thousand feet from a catastrophic crash.

Desperation fueled Josh's mind. "We need to get to the cockpit!" he yelled. "Maybe we can help the pilots!"

Amelia nodded, her face pale but determined. "Let's go!"

Fighting against the turbulent swaying of the plane, the trio made their way toward the cockpit. The passage was strewn with injured passengers and debris. As they reached the door, they found it locked and barricaded.

"Help us! We can assist!" Josh pounded on the door, hoping the pilots could hear him over the pandemonium.

The door cracked open, and the aircraft engineer, bloodied and frantic, peeked out. "Get back to your seats, now!" he ordered, forcing them away and back into the main cabin.

Frustrated but obedient, the trio returned to their seats, buckling in and holding on as the plane continued its rapid descent. The nightstalkers' assault showed no signs of relenting.

As land came into sight, the pilots hurled the plane toward the ground, attempting an emergency landing. The aircraft smashed onto the snowy terrain of Kamchatka, Soviet Union, skidding and creaking as it slowed to a halt. The violent impact split the plane in half, leaving the tail section about fifteen yards away from the main body.

Amelia, dizzy from the crash landing, woke up in the wrecked plane. Dazed, she unbuckled her seatbelt and stumbled out into the frigid air. The biting cold and the shock of the crash momentarily numbed her senses. As she took in her surroundings, she heard the ominous sound of a gun cocking, followed by angry shouting in Russian.

"Руки вверх!" a soldier yelled, the barrel of his rifle aimed squarely at her. Amelia's hands shot up instinctively, her heart pounding. She found herself surrounded by a group of Soviet soldiers, their faces stern and suspicious, clearly mistaking them for spies.

Amelia scanned the scene, spotting Emma and Josh emerging from the wreckage, equally disoriented and scared. The soldiers quickly corralled them, their weapons drawn and voices barking orders.

"Мы не шпионы!" Josh tried to explain, his limited Russian failing to convey the urgency of their situation. "Мы тут... эм... с гуманитарной помощью!"

One of the soldiers, seemingly in charge, stepped forward. His expression was skeptical as he scrutinized the trio. "Почему вы здесь?" he demanded.

Desperately, Emma pointed to the remnants of the UN markings on their clothing. "UN! We are with the United Nations!" she pleaded, hoping the recognition would buy them some time and understanding.

The leader of the soldiers raised an eyebrow, motioning for his men to lower their weapons slightly. He gestured for them to follow him, indicating they would be taken to a nearby facility for further questioning.

As they trudged through the snow, Amelia whispered to Josh, "We need to find a way to explain ourselves. They have to believe us."

Josh nodded, his mind racing. "We have the idol. If we can show them and explain its significance, maybe they'll understand."

Emma, walking beside them, added, "And we need to make sure Dominic doesn't get his hands on it again. Whatever it takes."

The soldiers led them to a makeshift outpost, where they were placed under guard. Their fate now depended on their ability to convince the Soviet authorities of their true intentions and the urgency of their mission. The trio knew they had to act quickly, not just to save themselves, but to protect the world from the escalating threat of the nightstalkers.

Seated in handcuffs in separate rooms, the trio found themselves under intense scrutiny from the skeptical Soviet soldiers. Each of them faced a stern interrogator, demanding to know their true purpose of arrival in the Soviet Union.

Josh, nervously sweating and struggling against the tight handcuffs, tried to explain their dire situation. "We made a crash landing because of the nightstalkers," he said, his voice shaking.

His movements alarmed the soldiers, prompting them to raise their guns at him. "Calm down!" one of the soldiers barked, his finger tightening on the trigger.

Suddenly, the door to Josh's room opened, and a soldier walked in, holding the idol. He spoke rapidly in Russian to the interrogating officer. The moment Josh saw the idol, his eyes widened with a mix of anger and desperation.

"HEY, GIVE IT BACK!" Josh shouted, trying to stand up and move towards the soldier. The idol represented their hope and the key to stopping the nightstalkers, and he couldn't afford to lose it now.

The soldier holding the idol quickly stepped back, while the interrogator shoved Josh back into his chair with a firm hand. "SHUT UP!" the soldier screamed, his patience wearing thin. The room filled with tense silence, everyone on edge.

Meanwhile, in the other rooms, Amelia and Emma were facing similar intense questioning. Amelia tried to remain calm and composed, explaining in her best Russian the nature of their humanitarian mission and the crash. "Мы правда с гуманитарной помощью," she insisted, her eyes pleading with the soldier to believe her.

Emma, on the other hand, used her knowledge of Soviet procedures and recent history to build a rapport with her interrogator. "Мы хотим помочь. Пожалуйста, поймите," she said, emphasizing their peaceful intentions and the importance of their mission.

Back in Josh's room, the soldier holding the idol placed it on the table in front of the interrogator. The officer studied it closely, his expression shifting from skepticism to curiosity. He looked back at Josh, his eyes narrowing. "Что это за штука?" he demanded, pointing to the idol.

Josh took a deep breath, trying to calm his racing heart. "That... that idol is what Dominic Blaze wants. He's using it to control the nightstalkers. If you don't believe us, the world is in grave danger. We're trying to stop him and save everyone."

The officer's eyes flickered with doubt and suspicion. He turned to the soldier who brought the idol and exchanged a few words in Russian. The soldier nodded and left the room.

After Josh explained the significance of the idol, the soldiers exchanged confused glances, murmuring amongst themselves. "Idol?" one of them repeated, furrowing his brow.

"Что за идол?" another soldier asked, clearly puzzled.

The officer who had been interrogating Josh turned to him again, his skepticism evident. "You expect us to believe that this... idol controls monsters?"

Josh nodded earnestly. "Yes, it's true. It's been used by Dominic Blaze to unleash the nightstalkers. We have to stop him, and this idol is the key."

One of the soldiers punched Josh in the stomach, causing him to double over in pain. "Лжец!" the soldier hissed.

Josh gasped, trying to catch his breath. "I'm not lying," he managed to say between pained breaths. "Please, you have to believe me."

The soldiers looked at each other again, the word "idol" still sounding foreign and implausible to them. One of them finally spoke up. "Если это правда, мы должны проверить."

The officer sighed, rubbing his temples. "We will see," he muttered. "But if this is a lie, it will be the end for you."

With that, he gestured for the soldiers to take Josh and the others out of the interrogation rooms. As they stood up, one of the soldiers punched Josh again, this time in the face, leaving him with a bruised cheek.

They were led back into a central holding area, where Amelia and Emma were already waiting, similarly disoriented and worried.

"We're going to show them the truth," Josh whispered to his friends, trying to sound more confident than he felt. "We have to."

His face was aching, and he could feel the blood trickling from the corner of his mouth, but he knew they had no choice but to prove their story was real.

With a menacing demeanor, the soldiers entered the room, their presence exuding authority and control. "Follow us," they commanded, their tone brooking no defiance. Amelia, her voice tinged with urgency, demanded answers, "Where are you taking us?" However, their interrogators remained steadfast, dismissing their explanations with contempt. "We don't believe your absurd story," one of the guards sneered, his words dripping with skepticism, "you will all be transported to a concentration camp."

"No!" Josh's protest erupted in a desperate plea, but his attempts to resist were met with brutal force. He found himself overwhelmed by the soldiers' relentless onslaught, enduring a barrage of blows from fists, boots, and rifle stocks. As he struggled against his assailants, Emma too faced the brunt of their aggression, her protests silenced by a merciless kick to the stomach.

Defeated and subdued, they were herded into a waiting truck along with the other survivors from the plane crash. Bound and helpless, they could do nothing but watch in dismay as the vehicle lurched into motion, its destination shrouded in ominous uncertainty.

XI

Kamchatka Labour Camp

The truck jolted to a stop after hours of relentless travel, and the soldiers wasted no time in herding the prisoners out. "Двигайтесь, черви!" they barked, punctuating their orders with harsh blows from their weapons. Josh, Amelia, and Emma were forcibly separated, each led to different corners of the desolate camp, a bleak landscape dominated by coils of barbed wire, looming fences, and watchful guard towers.

Josh found himself stripped of dignity, his head shorn and his body clad in a tattered prison uniform. Forced into grueling labor amid the biting cold, he endured a ceaseless barrage of abuse from both guards and fellow inmates alike. As he trudged wearily with a shovel slung over his shoulder, a soldier beckoned him aside, his voice tinged with an unexpected note of sympathy.

"I'm Dimitri... yes, from Vladivostok," he whispered, his words laden with secrecy, "I'm going to help you escape.

I know where your comrades are. Don't worry. Now, I'll pretend to strike you for pausing. Groan in pain."

As the relentless march of time dragged on in the desolate camp, Dimitri surreptitiously slipped a letter into Josh's hand. The hastily scrawled message conveyed a plan fraught with risk and hope:

"Listen, I got plan. U pretend dead 8 o clock, like real, ya know? Then they think u gone and toss u out. My buddy, Azaliya, gonna be there to pick u up. When she says 'Poydem', u get movin' and follow her. She gonna get u outta here in chopper. Chuck this note after, no evidence."

Josh read the words with a mix of trepidation and excitement, the promise of freedom beckoning tantalizingly within reach.

As 8 o'clock rolled around, Josh followed the plan to the tee. He dropped to the ground and held his breath, mimicking death as the soldier behind him prodded him with his boot, then gave him a whack on the noggin with his rifle. "Dead!" the soldier hollered to the supervisor in Russian. In no time, Josh found himself unceremoniously tossed out of the camp, left to freeze in the unforgiving snow. Staying true to his act, Josh lay still, waiting for Azaliya's arrival.

Minutes ticked by like eternity until he heard footsteps approaching, accompanied by a woman's voice. "Poydem!" she whispered urgently, signaling him to rise. With her guidance, Josh stumbled toward a distant CH-47 Chinook adorned with American insignia. Boarding the aircraft, Azaliya wrapped him in a thermal blanket, instructing him to wait inside. As he waited, a shadowy figure approached the chopper. The door swung open, revealing Amelia and Emma, battered and trembling from the cold.

Azaliya hustled onto the helicopter, barking orders at the pilots to take off. With a roar, the chopper ascended into the sky, its trajectory aimed toward the American mainland. "The idol!" Amelia's cry pierced the air as she stirred, recovering from a blow to the head delivered by a soldier's boot. She peered down at the diminishing camp below.

"No worries, no worries! I've got it!" Azaliya reassured them, producing the idol from a concealed compartment beneath the seat.

"What about the others?" Emma's voice trembled with concern. "What will happen to them?"

Azaliya paused, contemplating how best to deliver the news. With a heavy sigh, she replied, "Unfortunately, we weren't able to rescue any of them. They either perished before the plan could be executed or were apprehended when they played dead."

"As the aircraft continued on its course to the USA, Azaliya kept glancing at her watch, which made Amelia suspicious. "She seems pretty preoccupied," Amelia remarked to Emma and Josh, who were still recovering from their injuries.

"Well, guys, happy 1983!" Azaliya suddenly exclaimed, perplexing the group. "Wha- What?" Josh exclaimed in confusion. "It's the new year, guys! Cheer up!" Azaliya replied with enthusiasm. "Wait, how long have we been here?" Amelia inquired. "You all arrived on the 23rd of December," Azaliya informed them, prompting Josh to exclaim, "WE MISSED CHRISTMAS?!" The three of them exchanged annoyed glances with Azaliya before replying, "Missing Christmas is the least of our worries right now!"

XII

Home

As the Chinook neared the town of Crestwood, relieved parents gathered to embrace their children, leading to a heartwarming reunion. Yet, their concerns lingered, knowing they still had to confront Dominic and the sinister forces at the temple to ensure lasting safety.

"Could you take us to the temple in your helicopter?" Josh inquired of Azaliya, hoping for her support. Regrettably, she declined, explaining, "My duty was solely to return you home safely. I'm afraid I can't offer further assistance." With that, she boarded the helicopter, which ascended into the sky and departed for another destination.

Josh's indignant outcry reverberated through the air, tinged with frustration at the thought of trekking the distance once more. His remark prompted Amelia resounding slap landing on his head.

Subsequently, she glanced at Josh's parents, her expression seeking validation for her disciplinary measure. With an amused twinkle in his eye, Josh's father dismissed any notion of objection, asserting, "Don't look at me; I think he deserved it after that statement!" punctuating his statement with a hearty chuckle.

As they all made their way back home, reports of escalating attacks worldwide persisted. "There's been a notable surge in the frequency and severity of attacks globally," the news broadcast announced. "The scope of these assaults has expanded dramatically, with entire nations now falling prey to these relentless creatures. Overnight, they ravaged through New Zealand, Australia, all African countries south of the DRC, and the entirety of South America. The estimated death toll from last night's onslaught stands at 1.2 million, with authorities expecting it to rise as more casualties are uncovered."

XIII

The Forest

"Alright," Emma declared solemnly, laying out a map on the table before them. "This is our target: the temple." Her tone was resolute, reflecting the gravity of their mission. "The authorities have cordoned off both the main entrance and the access point through the waterfall, so we'll need to find an alternative route." With a steady hand, she traced a path around the rugged mountains, indicating their journey's circuitous path that would lead them to the temple's rear.

"We depart tomorrow," Josh declared with a sense of urgency. "Prepare your gear and supplies, because I have a feeling this time it's going to be more challenging."

As dawn broke, the team gathered at their designated meeting point, ready to embark on their journey. They trudged through the forest all day, the sun setting as they continued to their destination. With practiced efficiency, they set up their camp, securing their tents and starting a fire for warmth.

Standing watch outside, Josh felt the weight of exhaustion pressing down on him, but he remained vigilant. Suddenly, a crimson hue bathed the sky, accompanied by eerie screeches in the distance. Startled awake, Josh hurried into the tent, waking Amelia and Emma with urgency.

"He's onto us!" he exclaimed, his voice tight with apprehension as they emerged from the tent. They looked up at the ominous red sky, the air heavy with tension as hundreds of glowing eyes surrounded them.

Without hesitation, the nightstalkers charged, their terrifying screeches filling the air. "The flashlights!" Amelia shouted, distributing them to her companions as they prepared to defend themselves.

The nightstalkers recoiled as the bright beams of light pierced the darkness, but their victory was short-lived. Another wave descended upon them, wreaking havoc on their campsite before retreating into the shadows once more, leaving the group shaken but determined to press on.

As the sky returned to its usual hue, the group was left shaken by the encounter with the nightstalkers. "We need better protection against them," Emma stated, her mind already working on a solution. "Remember when a nightstalker charged at me four years ago and my cross pendant scared it?" she recalled.

"But we don't have the cross. How do we recreate that?" Josh asked, his brow furrowed in thought.

"Don't worry, guys, I have a solution!" Amelia exclaimed, a spark of excitement in her eyes. "I have a pouch with some glue, sandpaper, thin ropes, and some paper. We can glue some twigs together, sand them down, and fashion them into a makeshift cross. Then, we can attach a rope and wear it for protection!"

Emma and Josh exchanged a bemused glance before turning their attention back to Amelia. "Why do you carry all that?" they both asked simultaneously, their expressions a mixture of curiosity and confusion.

"Anyway, you two go to sleep. It's my turn to keep watch now," Amelia declared, settling near their sleeping bags as their tent lay in ruins.

When Josh stirred from his sleep the next morning and emerged from his sleeping bag, he found Amelia sitting nearby, her head slumped forward, and crafting supplies scattered around her. He gently nudged her, and she stirred, still groggy. "Oh... uh..." she mumbled, rubbing her eyes, "uh, um, here... I made these last night." She handed two crosses to Josh, one for Emma.

"You didn't sleep last night?" Josh asked, concern evident in his voice, but by then, Amelia was already dozing off again. "I think I got my answer," Josh remarked, with a hint of humor in his tone.

XIV

The Temple Of Shadows

After days of a perilous journey through the mountains and the jungle, the trio finally rounded the mountains, finally spotting the crumbled ruins of the temple. "Gosh darn it!" Josh whispered, pushing Amelia and Emma behind a tree. "Even the back is stiff with police!" he remarked, peeking cautiously from behind the tree.

"What should we do?" he asked urgently, receiving no immediate response. "Guys, what should we do??" he repeated, growing more anxious. Still met with silence, he turned to find Emma and Amelia gazing at the sky, their expressions filled with terror. The sky had turned crimson red once more, accompanied by the eerie sound of screeches. "B-but it's daytime!" Emma exclaimed in disbelief.

As she spoke, a bullet whizzed past them, followed by a familiar voice. "We meet again..." Dominic stood before them, aiming a gun with a menacing grip. "You thought just because you escaped from the Soviet Union, you were safe?" he taunted, his tone dripping with malice. "Hand me the idol, and we can forget all of this happened. You three can be my secretaries," he continued, extending his arm expectantly.

"Nah, we're good," Amelia retorted, tossing the idol to Josh, who stood behind Dominic. "Get him!" Dominic ordered, and a horde of nightstalkers rushed toward Josh. Ignoring the chaos around him, Josh sprinted toward the temple, his heart pounding with adrenaline.

As Josh reached the rubble of the temple, he frantically searched for the raised platform where the idol belonged. Meanwhile, the police officers, startled by the approaching nightstalkers, unleashed a barrage of bullets. However, their efforts were futile, as the bullets merely passed through the ethereal beings, who charged forward relentlessly.

"Found it!" Josh exclaimed triumphantly as he finally located the raised platform. But before he could place the idol, a sudden force sent him hurtling into the rubble, crashing down amidst the debris. Standing over him was a nightstalker, who retrieved the idol and handed it to Dominic with a sinister grin.

Unaware of Josh's predicament, Amelia and Emma cautiously approached Dominic, only to be swiftly tackled by the nightstalkers. "Thanks, guys," Dominic sneered, as they nightstalkers pinned down the helpless trio, his victory seeming inevitable.

"Why isn't the cross working?!" Amelia thought frantically, feeling a sense of desperation creeping in. Suddenly, Dominic's mocking voice interrupted her inner turmoil. "Oh, if you're wondering where your crosses are, they're safe with me," he taunted, holding up the crosses as proof.

Amelia's heart sank, realizing their last line of defense had been compromised. But she refused to give up hope. Summoning all her strength, she struggled against the nightstalker restraining her, her fingers fumbling for her flashlight. With a surge of determination, she managed to disorient the creature, creating a brief moment of respite.

Seizing the opportunity, Amelia acted swiftly, lunging forward to reclaim the idol. However, her triumph was short-lived as Dominic swiftly trained his gun on her, his expression twisted with malice. Caught in a precarious standoff, Amelia found herself held at gunpoint, her every move watched closely by her ruthless adversary.

"Don't move!" the police shouted, their voices filled with urgency as they raised their guns at Dominic, ready to apprehend him. However, their attempts were swiftly silenced as Dominic issued a chilling command to the nightstalkers, who ruthlessly dispatched the entire unit before they could react.

Amidst the chaos, Amelia summoned every ounce of her strength, determined to reach the platform and secure the idol. Despite Dominic's best efforts to thwart her, she persisted, even as a bullet pierced her flesh, causing her to collapse in pain. With sheer determination, she managed to place the idol on the platform just as the sky returned to its natural blue hue, dispelling the nightmarish creatures and granting freedom to Josh and Emma.

But victory came at a cost. Clutching her wounded leg, Amelia bravely stepped aside, urging Josh and Emma to proceed. However, Dominic seized the opportunity, holding Amelia at gunpoint and threatening her life.

With a determined and mysterious gesture, Josh picked the idol back up, summoning the Nightstalkers once more. The malevolent creatures now stood beside him, awaiting his command. "Kill him," Josh ordered, his eyes locked onto Dominic with unwavering resolve and revenge.

In an instant, the Nightstalkers growled and surged forward, their movements swift and deadly. They descended upon Dominic, delivering swift and merciless justice. The air was filled with the sounds of Dominic's desperate struggle and the Nightstalkers' growls, but it was over quickly.

With the deed done, Josh carefully returned the idol to its place, causing the sky to revert from its ominous crimson hue to its serene, natural state. The oppressive atmosphere lifted, and calm began to settle over the temple ruins.

As the dust settled, Josh reverently returned the idol to its rightful place, restoring peace to the temple grounds and signaling the end of Dominic's reign of terror. Soon, the distant sound of approaching helicopters heralded the arrival of rescue, marking the triumphant conclusion of their harrowing journey.

XV
The End

Amidst the clamor of helicopter rotors and the wail of police sirens in the distance, the group turned their attention to the approaching convoy. As the vehicles came to a stop near the temple, a flurry of activity ensued, with armed forces and paramedics rushing to their aid.

Upon finally arriving home in Crestwood, the group was met by a swarm of reporters from around the world, all eager to hear their story.

Despite her ordeal, Amelia made a full recovery in the hospital, her wounds gradually healing over time. In the days that followed, the group found comfort in the knowledge that they had defeated the nightstalkers once and for all, allowing them to finally rest, their mission complete.